Saturday Morning

Jennifer Romano

AuthorHouse™
1663 Liberty Drive
Bloomington, IN 47403
www.authorhouse.com
Phone: 1-800-839-8640

First published by AuthorHouse 1/4/2011

ISBN: 978-1-4520-0165-4 (sc)

Library of Congress Control Number: 2010907342

Printed in the United States of America
Bloomington, Indiana

This book is printed on acid-free paper.

authorHOUSE®

For Joe and Shannon, my everything, and my unknown.
I keep thinking it can't get any better than this...and it does.
Thank you for so much joy.

"Papa, what's Mimi doing?"

"Shhh...Mimi is sleeping, Buddy."

"Can we wake her up?"
"Why would we want to do that, Buddy?"

"Because I want to do something with you guys."

Papa folded his newspaper, set it aside, and asked, "What would you like to do?"

"I already told you, just something." Buddy said.

Then Papa asked, "Is it important?"

"Yes, it is to me."

"Well, tell me what it is, Buddy."

This time Buddy tried expressing himself with his hands as well as his voice, "I said, just something!"

Sensing Buddy's sincerity, Papa tried to keep things chipper.

"Hmmm...let's see if we can figure this out before we wake up Mimi," he said, lifting Buddy onto the chair.

"Let me guess...would you like to eat a roast beef dinner?"

"No Papa, I'm not hungry for dinner. We just ate pancakes!"
"All right then...how would you like to watch football on TV?"
asked Papa.

"I don't think Mimi likes football too much."
"Good point. Then we probably shouldn't wake her for that."

Papa continued to razz Buddy and called out, "I know, you want to vacuum the living room, right?"
"No thank you," said Buddy, shaking his head.

"I think I might be out of guesses. Wait, I have one more, but...
it couldn't possibly be..."
"What, Papa?"
"Could it be that you want to work on this year's income tax
return?"

"No way, Papa! I don't even know what that is!"
"Then what is it, Buddy? What would you like to do?"
Buddy sighed, "I just want to spend time with you guys, that's all."

"Oh...now I understand," said Papa. "I do believe Mimi would want us to wake her up for that. She loves spending time together. Maybe she will even have an idea of what we can do. Go ahead, see if you can wake her up."

Moving in close, Buddy whispered in her ear, "Wake up, Mimi."
Mimi tried not to giggle.

A little confused, Buddy looked at Papa, shrugged his shoulders, and looked back at Mimi.

This time Buddy carefully lifted Mimi's eyelid and whispered a little softer than before, "Wake up, Mimi. Wake up."

Slowly, Mimi opened her eyes, and while wearing a very big grin, she said in her sleepy voice, "Well, hello there, Buddy." "Hi, Mimi," he replied. Then he asked her quietly, "Would you like to spend some time with us?"

"As a matter of fact, that happens to be one of my favorite things to do," Mimi said. "How about we take a look at a photo album?"
"Sure!" Buddy and Papa said at the same time.
"Okay, I will go and get it from the bookshelf," said Mimi.

"No you stay here, Mimi, I will get it!" Buddy said
enthusiastically. Then he sprang up and went over to the
bookshelf.

He pointed to a book, and asked, "Is this it?"
"That's it!" Papa said. "You got it."

"Yep, I got it."
Buddy started to pull on the book. It was wedged in tight.

He groaned as he pulled with all his might, stumbling backwards when the book came free.

Instinctively, Mimi leaned forward and began to reach out. "Do you need help Buddy?" She was silently reassured by Papa's hand patting her shoulder.

"No, I don't need help, because I have muscles." Buddy stopped what he was doing, posed in such a way that would best show off his biceps, and said, "See my muscles."

"Whoa. Those are quite impressive!" Mimi stated, settling back into the chair.

"Okay, Muscles, come on up here," Papa said, boosting Buddy and the tightly clutched book onto the chair.

Then they all snuggled in with the book on their laps.

Before opening the book, Buddy turned to Mimi and asked,
"Why do people take pictures?"
"Because looking at pictures helps people remember the
special moments in their lives," Mimi answered.
"I think this is a special moment," said Buddy.

"You know what, Buddy, I think you are right. In fact, it seems like this Saturday morning has been full of special moments, and right now…we are smack dab in the middle of one." Papa replied. "Your Mimi and I wish there was a way we could remember this forever."

Just then a cheery voice called out from upstairs. "Hello? Is there anyone here?"
Papa yelled back, "We are all downstairs. Come on down."

It was Buddy's mom and dad. "Hey Buddy! How are you doing?" they asked.
"Good, but I'm not ready to go home yet. Can we stay a little bit longer and look at the picture book? Please?"

"Absolutely," said Buddy's dad. "We can stay as long as you like or...until eight o'clock, whichever comes first."

They looked at the photo album, and as they turned the pages of baby pictures, birthdays, weddings, and holidays, they shared their stories.

Their memories of the past merged with their dreams for the future, and it filled their hearts with a closeness that connected everything into this one moment.

When they were finished, Buddy turned to his mom and asked, "Mom, will you take a picture of me with Mimi and Papa, so they can remember our special moment forever?"
"It would be my pleasure, Bud."

She pulled the camera out of her purse, aimed it at her family, and said, "Say cheese!"

The End

LaVergne, TN USA
21 March 2011
R6075700001B